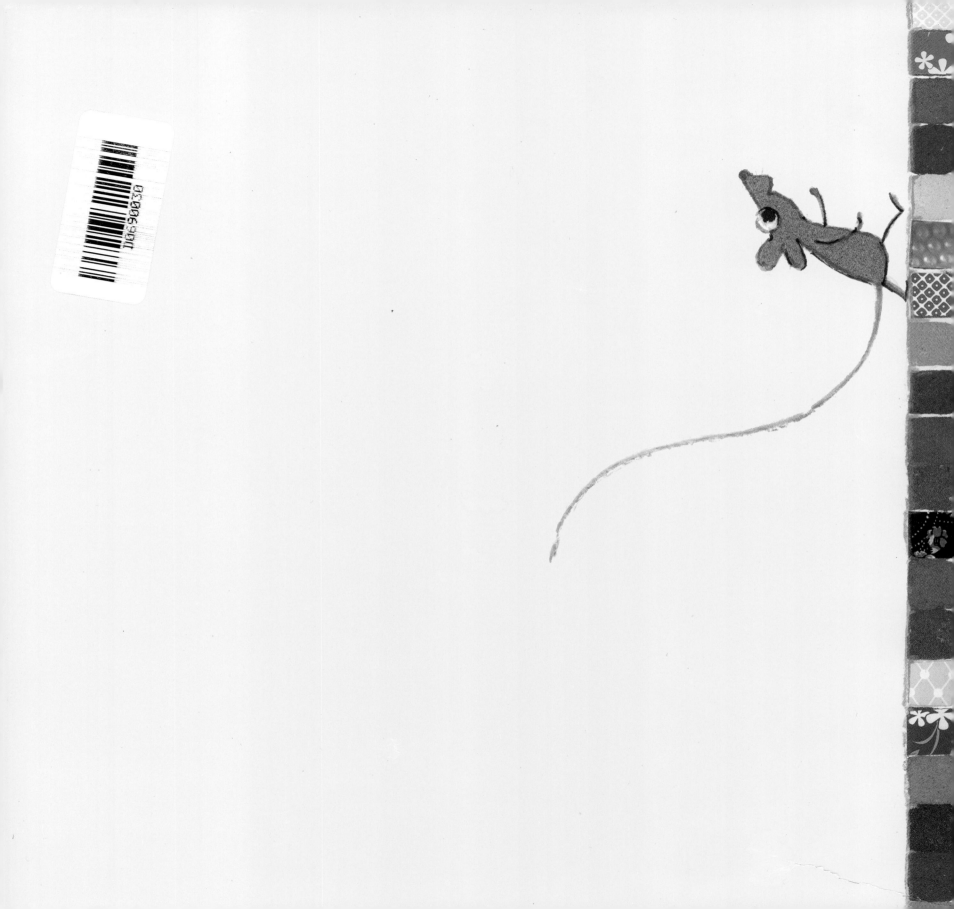

Give a **SHOUT** for Dr. Steven Gale!

Henry Holt and Company, LLC
Publishers since 1866
175 Fifth Avenue
New York, New York 10010
www.HenryHoltKids.com

Henry Holt® is a registered trademark
of Henry Holt and Company, LLC.
Copyright © 2011 by Denise Fleming
All rights reserved.
Distributed in Canada by H. B. Fenn and Company Ltd.

Library of Congress Cataloging-in-Publication Data
Fleming, Denise.
Shout! Shout it out! / Denise Fleming. — 1st ed.
p. cm.
Summary: Mouse invites the reader to shout out what
he or she knows as they review numbers, letters,
and easy words.
ISBN 978-0-8050-9237-0
[1. Mice—Fiction. 2. Alphabet—Fiction. 3. Numbers,
Natural—Fiction. 4. Vocabulary—Fiction.] I. Title.
PZ7.F5994Sho 2011 [E]—dc22   2010011691

First Edition—2011
Printed in December 2010 in China by C&C
Joint Printing Co., Shenzhen, Guangdong
Province, on acid-free paper. ∞

10 9 8 7 6 5 4 3 2 1

Visit www.denisefleming.com.

The illustrations were created by pulp painting—a papermaking technique using colored cotton fiber poured through hand-cut stencils. Accents were added with patterned paper collage, pastel pencil, china marker, and colored indian inks.
Book design by Denise Fleming and David Powers.

SHOUT! Shout it out!

Denise Fleming

Henry Holt and Company • New York

You're pretty.

Everybody loves to shout. So, if you know it,

SHOUT it it out! Ready. Set. *Go!*

Four!

I like your bow.

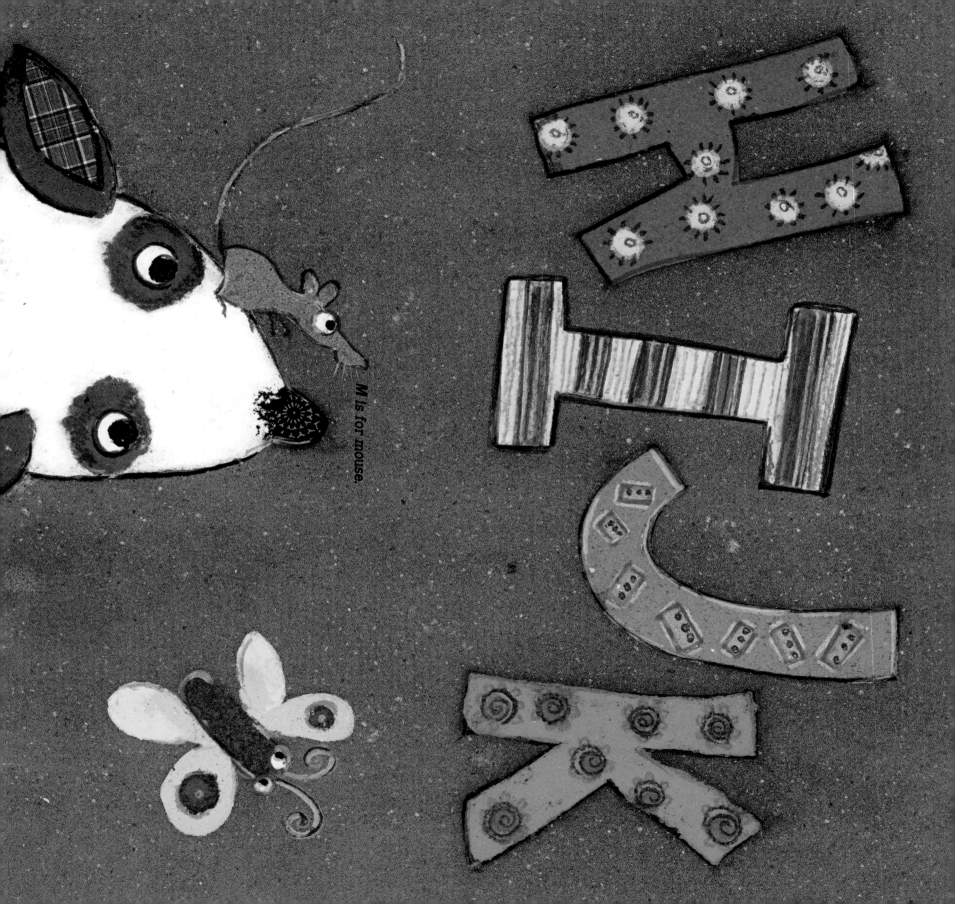

M is for mouse.

SHOUT! SHOUT! SHOUT!

Shout it out!

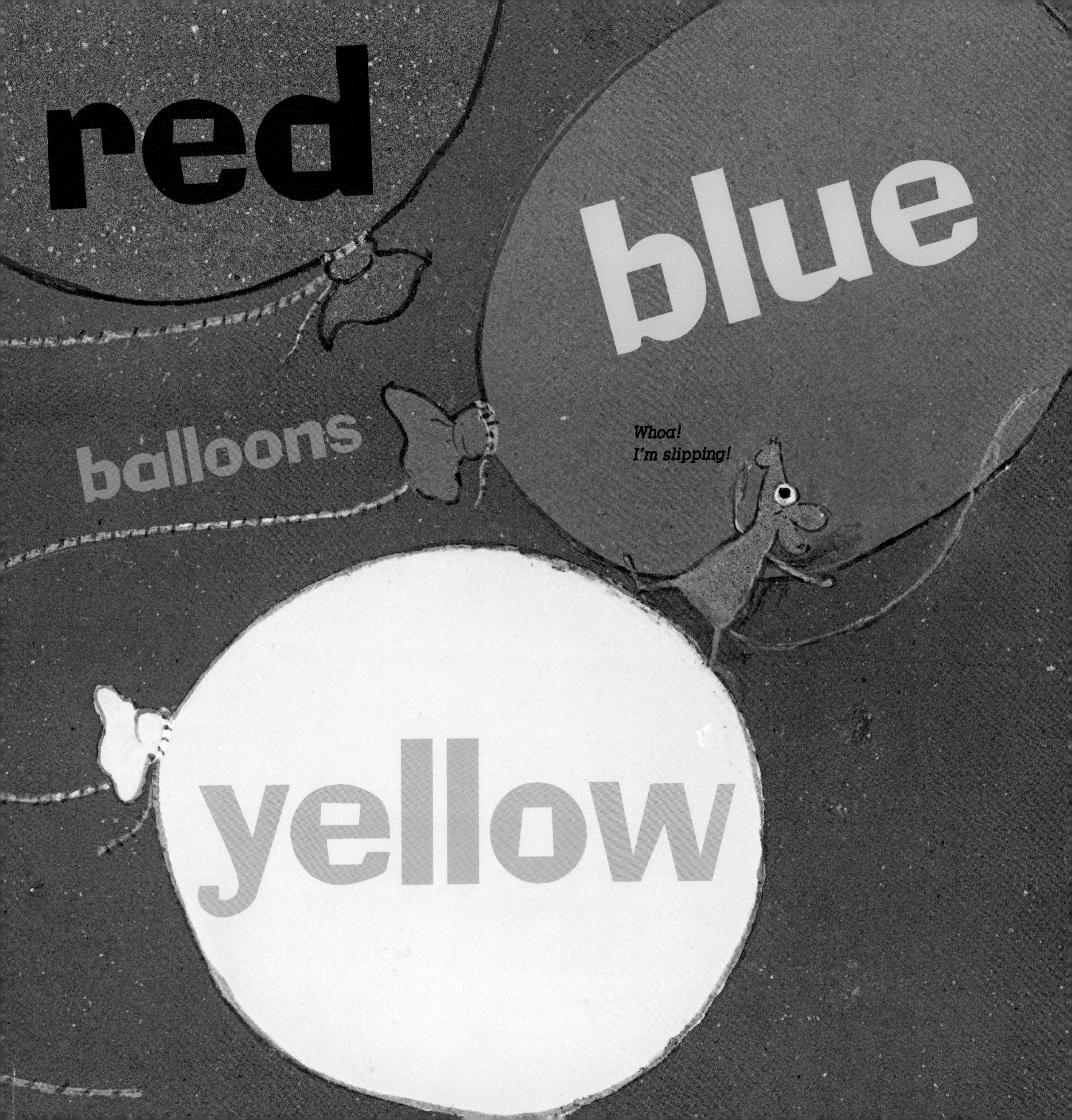
red
blue
balloons
Whoa!
I'm slipping!
yellow

greeen

balloons

purple

orange purple

Purple is my favorite color.

Mouse.

cat

hamster

SHOUT! SHOUT!
Shout it out!

bird

rabbit

dog

COW

duck

flies

I draw flies. Ha ha.

pig

chicken

goat

Giddy up!

sheep

bees

horse

car

SHOUT! SHOUT! SHOUT!

Shout it out!

boat

bus

Wait for me!

truck

Blow your horn!

plane

train

Mouse, tell us what you know.

A B C D E F G

O P Q R S T

1 2 3 4 5 6 7 8 9 10

cat bird dog rabbit hamster

cow flies duck chicken pig

goat horse bees sheep

Ready. Set. *Go!*

HIJKLMN

UVWXYZ

red blue yellow purple

green orange balloons

car bus truck plane train boat

Well done!

Thank you.